SUPERBIRD TO THE RESCUE

NANCY HAYASHI

SUPERBIRD TO THE RESCUE

DUTTON CHILDREN'S BOOKS • NEW YORK

Copyright © 1995 by Nancy Hayashi
Library of Congress Cataloging-in-Publication Data
Hayashi, Nancy. Superbird to the rescue /
by Nancy Hayashi.—1st ed.   p.   cm.
Summary: Jesse Beeman is always involving his best friend,
Walter Fujikawa, in his crazy ideas, but things get out of hand
when they take Jesse's pet parrot to the mall to try
to catch shoplifters.   ISBN 0-525-45198-6
[1. Parrots—Fiction. 2. Pets—Fiction.]
I. Title.   PZ7.H313874Su   1995
[Fic]—dc20 94-20464 CIP AC
Published in the United States
by Dutton Children's Books,
a division of Penguin Books USA Inc.
375 Hudson Street, New York, New York 10014
Designed by Adrian Leichter
Printed in U.S.A.
First Edition
1   3   5   7   9   10   8   6   4   2

IN MEMORY OF
THE DWIRE SISTERS—
LUCILLE, ISABELLE, JANETTE,
AND VIRGINIA

C O N T E N T S

SUPERBIRD TO THE RESCUE

STUPID LUCAS

W hat do you mean it's not going to work?" Jesse Beeman said. "It's going to be so *easy*." Jesse and his best friend, Walter Fujikawa, were on their way home from school. Jesse was telling Walter about his newest idea. They were going to teach Zenith how to type. Zenith was Jesse's parrot. The typing idea had hit Jesse suddenly during reading period. He hadn't been able to think of anything else since.

3

"All we have to do is put sunflower seeds on the typewriter keys, one at a time," said Jesse. "Zenith picks up the seed, her beak pushes down the key, and—bingo! She can peck out anything we want her to. Maybe we'll have her type a letter to somebody."

"I still don't think it's going to work," Walter said. "But I'll help you. My horoscope said today would be a good day for correspondence, and Mom says that means letter writing."

"It's a *great* day for it," said Jesse happily. "Maybe we can finish the letter before your mother comes." Walter stayed at Jesse's house every day after school until his mother picked him up on her way home from work.

When they reached Jesse's driveway, he raced ahead of Walter. Suddenly he stopped. He could hear his mother's voice calling Zenith.

"Shh." Jesse motioned to Walter. They tiptoed to the gate into the backyard and looked over it.

"Zenith's in the tree again," Jesse whispered. "Let's watch for a minute." He could see the flash of her bright green feathers as she climbed about the branches. She loved to rip off pieces of bark to chew on.

Although Jesse was in a hurry to start the typing lesson, he was glad Zenith was having fun. She spent too much time in the house, except on days like today when she managed to escape. Getting outside was good for a parrot. That's what Jesse kept telling his mother. It would be even better for Zenith if she could go outside with him. That would be wonderful. With her riding on his shoulder, he'd feel just like a pirate. They could go everywhere together. All sorts of exciting things would happen to the two of them.

Jesse sighed.

There was no use thinking about it. Whenever he asked his mother to let him take Zenith out somewhere, she refused. She said it might be too dangerous for a parrot.

They watched Mrs. Beeman put a handful of peanuts on a table under the tree in the backyard. Almost immediately, a chunk of bark hit the table and scattered the nuts. "What a nuisance you are," she grumbled as she bent over to pick them up.

"Come on down, Zenith. That's a good girl." Mrs. Beeman held up a peanut temptingly. Her voice was sweet and coaxing now. Just then a bigger piece of bark landed by her feet. Another bounced off her head. "Now stop that, Zenith! Bad bird!"

Jesse and Walter were laughing so hard they didn't hear Jesse's older brother, Lucas, come up behind them.

"What are you little shrimps doing?" Lucas

7

said, putting both hands on Jesse's shoulders and pushing down hard. He did that a lot lately—ever since he had started eighth grade. It always made Jesse angry.

"Cut it out, Lucas!" Jesse wriggled out of his grip.

Mrs. Beeman glanced over. "Thank heavens you're home. Come help me get this blasted bird down."

The boys unlatched the gate and shoved through. As soon as they were under the tree, they looked up to see what Zenith was doing. She had stopped nibbling the bark and was scolding herself happily. "Bad bird! Bad bird!" She was very good at imitating voices. It almost sounded as if Mrs. Beeman were up in the tree with her.

By now, the neighbor's dachshund, Sasha, had heard her and started to bark. Zenith barked back.

"How did she get out this time, Mom?" Jesse asked.

"I left the porch door open while I took some newspapers to the garage," Mrs. Beeman told him. "That door was open for no more than two minutes. And Zenith wasn't even on the porch. She was on the climbing tree in your room."

"Zenith always knows when the porch door is open," Jesse said proudly. "She has ears like a hawk."

Lucas laughed at him. "*Eyes* like a hawk, stupid."

"Who's stupid?" Jesse said hotly. He yelled up at Zenith, "Who's stupid?"

They heard a squawk from the top of the tree and then, "Stupid Lucas." Zenith had learned that from Jesse. It was the first thing he had taught her to say.

Lucas glared at Jesse. He had repeated "Jesse's a jerk" over and over, but Zenith never picked it up. Jesse could teach her anything, though. He was her favorite member of the family.

"Let's get Zenith down quickly," Mrs. Beeman urged. "She may take a notion to fly next door again, and you know she drives that dog crazy."

Sasha was barking furiously now.

"Hurry, before Mrs. Orewiler comes out."

But it was too late.

HELP, ZENITH!

Boys, is that vicious parrot of yours loose again?" Their neighbor, Mrs. Orewiler, was peeking over the fence. It was so high that she had to stand on top of a box. "You know, I'm not one to make trouble," she went on. "But if this keeps up, I may have to report your bird to the authorities."

That was what she had said the last time Zenith was outside. Jesse didn't know what she meant, but it worried him.

"Now I'll have to take Sasha inside before he's attacked again." Mrs. Orewiler clapped her hands. "Sasha!"

"Zenith won't hurt Sasha," Jesse said. "She only wants to play."

Mrs. Orewiler ignored him. "Sasha! Come here, Sasha!"

Zenith began calling, too. "Sasha! Sasha!"

Jesse giggled. It sounded as if their neighbor were up in the tree.

Mrs. Orewiler glared at him. "And it's a shame I won't be able to hang my sheets out—"

Mrs. Beeman cut in quickly. "Don't worry, Gladys. The boys are going to take her back inside right now." She knew why their neighbor had mentioned the sheets. So did Jesse. Last week, Zenith had picked all the clothespins off Mrs. Orewiler's clothesline, and her laundry had ended up on the ground.

"Why does she have to hang stuff out, any-way?" Jesse muttered to Walter. "Nobody else does."

"Come on, Jesse," Lucas said. "Let's get Zenith down." He grabbed Jesse by the arm and started to shake him.

"Owwwwowwww!" Jesse howled. "Help! Help!"

Walter watched Zenith as she began scooting back and forth on the branch. "She's starting to get excited," he reported. "Keep it up."

"Pow! Pow!" With his free hand, Lucas threw fake punches at Jesse, missing him by a few inches.

Zenith screeched, Sasha barked, and Jesse yelled as Lucas shook him harder and harder.

"OWW! OWWW!"

"What a disgraceful racket," Mrs. Orewiler complained, covering her ears.

Zenith looked much larger now, with her

feathers puffed out. She flapped her wings and slashed the air with her beak.

"You'd better get out of the way, Walter," Mrs. Beeman warned. Then she moved quickly to the back porch and held the screen door open.

"Help, Zenith!" Jesse yelled. "Save me from Lucas! Stupid Lucas!"

When he heard that, Lucas yanked Jesse's arm behind his back and pinned it there. Jesse's screams went several notches higher.

"Stop it!" Jesse twisted sideways and kicked Lucas in the ankle. They rolled over in a heap and thrashed around on the ground.

"That's enough, you two." Mrs. Beeman hurried over to them.

Just then, Zenith came dive-bombing out of the tree.

Now Lucas was the one doing the howling. "Get her off me! Quick!"

Zenith had clamped a hunk of his sweatshirt in her beak. Her wings were still flapping hard.

A startled yelp came from the fence. In all the excitement, Mrs. Orewiler had fallen off her box.

"Calm Zenith down, Jesse," said Mrs. Beeman. "I wish there were some other way to get that bird down," she grumbled as she hurried over to check on their neighbor.

"Come on, Zenith, let go. Let go," Jesse kept repeating as he pried her off Lucas. At last, she climbed up Jesse's arm to his shoulder. Her feathers were still puffed out and she glared fiercely at Lucas.

"Good old Zenith," Jesse said. He scratched Zenith's head as she began to nibble his ear.

"Look what good old Zenith did to me," Lucas complained. He fingered the hole she had made in his sweatshirt.

"It's your own fault," Jesse said. "You could have gotten away if you had just been *pretending* to beat me up."

Lucas didn't admit it, but he knew Jesse was right. The Beeman family had discovered there was only one way to coax Zenith down from the tree: Jesse and Lucas had to stage a fight. Then Zenith would come flying to Jesse's rescue. It worked every time, but Lucas had to move quickly to get out of her way.

Before Mrs. Orewiler went inside, she said something again about calling the authorities. Jesse heard her, but he was too happy to worry. He felt so proud of Zenith. No one else had such a wonderful pet.

He wanted to take her everywhere, if only his mother would let him. It would be great to go to school with Zenith on his shoulder. Jesse could see himself standing up to Nelson O'Connell, the biggest bully in his class. "Give me back that pencil case you took," he'd tell him. "Or else!" He wouldn't have to be afraid of Nelson. Zenith would protect him.

"Come on, Walter," Jesse said. "Superbird deserves a reward. There are some grapes in the refrigerator. Zenith loves grapes, and wait till you see how she eats them!"

"I know—you already told me." Walter trotted up the steps behind Jesse. "And I still don't believe you."

CHAPTER 3

TRIPLE-KNOTTED
TROUBLE

See, I told you she could do it." Jesse lay on his bed, tossing grapes over to Zenith. She was strutting around on top of his desk.

Walter was sprawled in a chair, watching her. Just as Jesse had claimed, she really was peeling the grapes with her beak. She was also squashing them and smearing the sticky pulp all over Jesse's desk.

"Look at her eyes," Walter said. "The black

parts get bigger and then smaller, bigger and smaller."

"They always do that when she's excited," Jesse said. "It makes her look crazy—sort of like a mad scientist."

Jesse jumped off the bed. "Let's get started typing that letter. I bet it will be the first letter ever typed by a parrot. If we send it to the newspaper, maybe they will print it. You'll be famous, Zenith."

Zenith hopped down to explore the open desk drawer. Waddling around inside, she tossed out pencils, erasers, and scrunched-up pieces of paper. "Hey, birdbrain. Happy New Year!" she chattered to herself. "Bad bird. Now stop that!"

Jesse grinned. "She sounds just like Mom."

"Stop that, Zenith!"

For a moment, Jesse thought Zenith was still talking. Then he saw his mother standing in the doorway. "Look at what your precious bird is doing," Mrs. Beeman said, shaking her head.

"She's making a nest," Jesse said. "Maybe Zenith thinks she's in a hollow log in the jungle. Dad says that's where wild parrots make their nests."

Mrs. Beeman laughed and said, "She's making more of a mess than a nest. Put her back in the cage now, Jesse. We're going to the shopping mall."

"Do we *have* to come with you?" Jesse asked.

"Yes, you do," she answered. "You need at least four pairs of new pants."

Just then, Zenith flew to her climbing tree on the other side of the room. The whirring of her wings blew even more paper scraps out of the drawer.

"I wish there was time to take Zenith to the pet shop at the mall," Mrs. Beeman said. "Her wing feathers need to be clipped again. Lately she's been flying up to places where I can't reach her—like the tree today." Mrs. Beeman left the room. "Don't forget to put Zenith in her cage," she called back.

Jesse coaxed Zenith down from her tree and put her back in the cage. "We'll never get that letter typed today," he grumbled. Then Jesse and Walter went downstairs and out to the garage.

Mrs. Beeman was already in the car waiting for them. "Your mother said you need a new jacket," she told Walter as he and Jesse got into the car. "She wants you to buy a red one. That way, you'll be able to find it more easily in the lost-and-found box at school."

"I haven't lost *that* many jackets," Walter said. "But red's okay. It's my lucky color." Walter put a great deal of faith in luck.

Jesse did not. "Ha!" he snorted. "Your bike was red, and it was stolen anyway."

"But it was more black than red," Walter objected. "Black is my *unlucky* color."

They reached the mall in ten minutes. It took almost that long to find a parking space.

Once inside Hayes Department Store, Jesse's mother picked out an armful of pants for him to try on. Jesse hated doing that. Shirts weren't so bad, but pants were too much trouble. He'd have to take off his shoes. That meant untying the double knots in his shoelaces. Oh no. He remembered that he had triple-knotted his laces that morning because they were too long.

Luckily, all the pants fit. He left his laces untied, though, just in case he had to try on more.

He slung the pants over his shoulder and left the dressing room. His mother and Walter were already at the cashier's counter. Walter looked happy. He had found a red jacket. "I bet I'll get an A in spelling tomorrow if I wear my new lucky jacket."

"Mrs. Lopez will make you take it off. She says we get sleepy when we're too hot," Jesse reminded him. They headed toward the escalator. "You sure were lucky today, though. All you had to try on was that jacket."

As they walked out the exit that led into the mall area, a loud siren went off.

"That's the store alarm," Mrs. Beeman told them. She looked around. They were the only people leaving the store.

"Did *we* do that?" asked Jesse excitedly. "I should have tied my shoes. We might have to make a run for it."

"Don't be silly, Jesse." Mrs. Beeman looked

flustered. The siren was still shrieking, and people were beginning to stare at them. "It must be a mistake," she said. "But I wonder if . . . Walter, let me see your new jacket."

Walter pulled his jacket out of the bag and handed it to her. There was a white plastic tag hanging from one sleeve.

"That's it. The saleswoman forgot to remove the tag, and it set off the alarm."

"My jacket did that?" Walter's voice squeaked. "They're going to think I stole it."

Just then, a man carrying a walkie-talkie hurried up to them. "Excuse me . . ." he began.

Mrs. Beeman's face was getting redder and redder as she hunted through her purse. She looked up and smiled at the man. "You must be the store detective."

"Yes, ma'am. One of them," he answered.

"Cool!" Jesse said and poked Walter. This

was great! It even made trying on all those pants seem worthwhile. He wished Walter would stop looking so worried.

"I know I have the receipt for the jacket in here somewhere. Oh, here it is." Mrs. Beeman handed the receipt to the detective.

He checked it and said, "Well, this looks all right to me. Sorry to have bothered you. If you go back into the store, someone will take the tag off."

They followed him in and went to the first saleswoman they saw. She snipped off the tag with a special tool.

"Does everything have a tag on it?" Jesse asked. He couldn't remember seeing them on his new pants.

"No, they are only on certain items," the saleswoman told him. "And lately, even these tags don't stop the shoplifters," she went on. "There's been one nearly every day."

Now Walter was interested. "What kind of things do they take?"

"Oh, anything you can think of. Last week, a woman walked out with a blanket wrapped around her, under her coat. It fell out when she was going down the escalator, but they still didn't catch her."

Jesse and Walter started laughing.

"Well, it's not funny," the saleswoman said. "A girl almost got away with four sets of earrings yesterday. She put her Walkman headphones on over them. Luckily, someone saw her do it."

On the way to the car, Jesse was full of excitement. He raced back and forth on the sidewalk, following the zigzag pattern of the bricks. He could tell he was about to get one of his terrific ideas.

"Settle down, Jesse," Mrs. Beeman said

crossly. "And tie your shoelaces, for heaven's sake."

It was nearly six o'clock, so Mrs. Beeman took Walter straight home. Halfway there, Jesse thought of it. "I just had an incredible idea, Walter."

Walter laughed. "Not another one," he said and ducked as Jesse aimed a punch at him.

"Just wait till you hear it," Jesse said. "It's the best idea I've ever had. I'll tell you tomorrow."

UND#RCOB$R AGEM¢S

So *tell* me," Walter said impatiently. All day he had been asking Jesse about his new idea. Jesse had told Walter he'd tell him after school. He loved to keep Walter in suspense.

Now it was after school, and they had just reached Jesse's house.

"As soon as we get to my room," Jesse promised.

They made a quick stop in the kitchen for

cookies and root beer. Then they raced up to Jesse's room.

Jesse stalled some more. "Wait a minute. I want to give this to Zenith." He always picked up new branches for Zenith to chew on. Today he had found one that was a perfect size.

"Let me out of here!" Zenith screeched when she saw him.

"Here you go, Superbird," Jesse said. He opened the cage and she climbed out and onto the branch. Then he wedged it firmly in his wastebasket.

Walter exploded. "What is this fantastic, terrific, incredible idea of yours?" He wasn't in a good mood. Mrs. Lopez hadn't let him wear his new lucky jacket, and he had flunked the spelling test. "Are you going to have Zenith type the whole Gettysburg Address, or what?"

Jesse looked startled. He had forgotten all about the typing. "No . . . it's a different idea." But now that Walter had reminded him, he hated to give the typing up completely. He thought for a moment.

"I know what Zenith can type—business cards. We're going to need them." Jesse grabbed a piece of paper and started to write. "Let's see . . . *Jesse Beeman and Walter Fujikawa* . . . *Store Detectives.*" He scratched out the last part. "*Undercover Agents.* That sounds better."

Walter started to ask a question, but Jesse rushed on. "Remember what the saleswoman said yesterday about the shoplifters? Well, we can catch them—I know we can."

"What do you mean?" Walter asked. "If we see people stealing, we report them?"

"Report them! No way," Jesse said scornfully. "We're going to catch them ourselves."

Walter nibbled a cookie. "Sounds dangerous to me. Shoplifters are probably a lot bigger than we are. We'd need some sort of protection."

"I've thought about that." Jesse took a quick gulp of root beer. This was his favorite part of the plan. "We've got the greatest protection ever, right here—Superbird!"

Zenith stopped chewing on the branch and chimed in. "Superbird! Hey, birdbrain."

"She'll go after anyone if I'm in danger," Jesse said proudly.

Walter laughed. "Well, folks, it's another crazy idea from Jesse Beeman."

"What's so crazy about it?" Jesse demanded.

"How are we going to get to the mall by ourselves?" Walter began. "And how can we take Zenith along? You know your mom will never let us."

"We can go with Lucas. That will be okay

with Mom." Jesse sounded confident. "And once we're there, we can ditch him." Jesse knew this wouldn't be hard to do. Lucas wouldn't want his friends to see him with his little brother. If they promised to meet Lucas later, he would let them go off on their own.

Walter looked doubtful, but Jesse thought that deep down he liked the idea. Walter picked up the paper with their names scribbled on it. He folded it to the size of a business card. "We should have our phone numbers on this," he said. Jesse knew he was hooked.

Jesse took another swallow of root beer. "I still haven't thought of a way to take Zenith along," he admitted. "While I figure out a plan, let's have Zenith type a business card. I'll see if Mom will let us borrow her typewriter."

Jesse opened his door and ran downstairs. In a few minutes he returned, lugging an old electric typewriter. Sunflower seeds dribbled from a bag he had stuffed under his arm.

"Mom said we can use this until Lucas needs it for his book report," Jesse panted. "Boy, is this typewriter *heavy*. We'll put it over there." He pointed to his desk.

Walter swept Jesse's backpack off the desk onto the floor. "So—how are we going to take Zenith to the mall?"

"I'm still thinking. Don't rush me." Jesse cranked a piece of paper into the typewriter. Zenith protested loudly when he took her off her new branch. "Now, stop that! Stop that!" she shrieked as she tried to fly back to it. Jesse caught her and set her down on the desk. He showed her the sunflower seeds. Next he plugged in the typewriter and turned it on. The machine hummed into life and then made a steady ticking noise. Zenith gave a squawk and backed away from it.

"Come on, Zenith. It won't hurt you," Jesse coaxed. He put one sunflower seed on the *j* key.

Walter looked at the carefully placed seed. "Wait a minute. Why is your name first?"

"*Somebody* has to be first. Besides, it's my idea, isn't it?" Seeing the stubborn look on Walter's face, Jesse gave in. "Okay, okay. On the next card we'll put your name first."

Zenith was still eyeing the typewriter suspiciously. At last, she couldn't resist. With a quick peck, the seed disappeared and a perfect *j* appeared on the paper.

Jesse gave a cheer. "Look at that!"

"It works, but it should be a capital *J*," Walter pointed out.

"You're right. Let me think. Mom showed me how to make capitals." Jesse studied the

keyboard for a moment. "I think you have to push these two buttons down. We'll make all the letters capitals."

He moved the paper to a new spot and put down another seed. Zenith snatched it up. This time, she typed a capital *J* and, after a few more seeds, an *E* and an *S*.

"Works perfectly now," Jesse said. Just then, Zenith's beak sideswiped the next *S* and hit the *Q*.

"*JESQ!*" Walter was laughing, but Jesse was not. After all, it was Jesse's name that was being messed up.

Jesse cranked the paper a few inches higher and started over. This time, Zenith only got as far as *JE* before hitting a *D*.

"JED!" Walter thought that was even funnier. "That's what I'll call you from now on." He waved his hand toward Jesse. "Folks, meet my good friend, Jed."

"Very funny." Jesse sounded grumpy. He moved the paper up again.

Zenith hit all the right letters until she reached the final *E*. Then she knocked a seed between the keys. Jesse tried to pick it out, but it was wedged tight.

"Your name is nothing but bad luck," Walter said. "Try mine first."

"Oh, all right," Jesse said. "This is taking too long. Let's use just our first names."

Three pieces of paper later, their best card read:

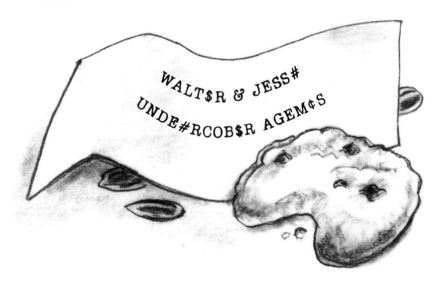

WALT$R & JESS#
UNDE#RCOB$R AGEM¢S

By now, there were a lot of seeds stuck between the keys. But what worried Jesse more was the root beer he had spilled all over the keyboard.

"This is never going to work. Come on, Walter. Help me clean up the typewriter before Lucas has to use it. He'll tell Mom I made a mess." Jesse picked at the seeds with a straightened-out paper clip.

Walter began to wipe the wet, sticky keys with the bottom of his T-shirt. "Have you thought of a way to take Zenith to the mall yet?" he asked.

"Who's had time to think?" said Jesse crossly. "But don't worry. I'll come up with something."

Zenith had lost interest in the sunflower seeds. Now she was pacing back and forth on the desk. Suddenly she took off. Flapping hard, she headed for her new branch.

Jesse stared at her for a moment. "I've got it!" he announced excitedly. "Didn't I tell you I'd think of something? We can take Zenith to the pet shop at the mall to get her wings clipped. Mom will let us do that. She says that Zenith is flying around the house and driving her crazy."

Jesse was happy now. He sniffed at the typewriter keys. There was still a scent of root beer about them. It was a nice smell, but he hoped his mother didn't notice it. "And we can get Lucas to take us on Friday, after school."

Walter was looking a little doubtful again. "Fridays are usually pretty lucky for me, but what if there aren't any shoplifters?"

"Don't worry," said Jesse. "There will be. Why, I'll bet you right now some woman is trying to sneak a mink coat out under her sweatshirt."

He could hardly wait till Friday. At last, he was going to do something exciting with Zenith. And Walter, too, of course.

SHOPLIFTERS BEWARE

Here you go, Zenith—popcorn, grapes, peanuts." Jesse dumped all of this on his bed. Then he handed Zenith a chicken leg with a little meat left on it. She held it with one foot and nibbled greedily.

"I want to build up her strength for tomorrow," Jesse told Walter.

"She's going to be too fat to fly," Walter said.

It was Thursday afternoon. They had to

45

make all their plans for Friday before Walter went home.

"I still say I'm going to need some sort of protection." Walter picked up a handful of peanuts. "Zenith won't defend *me* from shoplifters."

"I know, I know," Jesse said. They had argued about this on the way home from school. "I told you I'd think of something."

Jesse scratched Zenith's head. That always helped him to concentrate. "I've got it," he announced after a moment. "Pepper."

But Walter didn't get it, so Jesse had to explain. "When you blow pepper in someone's face, he can't do anything but sneeze. It's a great defense."

"Okay, I'll bring some pepper," said Walter. "And I'll wear my lucky hat."

"NO! Not your hat!" Jesse was alarmed. "We're *undercover* agents. We want to blend in with the crowd. Believe me, that hat won't blend." Walter's lucky hat was Day-Glo green with a red propeller on top.

"Oh, all right." Walter gave in. "I'll bring my horseshoe magnet instead. That's almost as lucky. And my fossil rock—the one with a mark like a four-leaf clover on it."

Jesse nodded. "But don't bring too much junk—I mean, lucky stuff," he said hastily, seeing the indignant look on Walter's face. "We want to be able to move fast."

Zenith dropped the chicken leg and fluttered to the top branch of her climbing tree. Nodding her head up and down, she demanded, "Popcorn, popcorn."

Jesse scooped some popcorn into a little bucket that hung on a chain from the branch. Zenith hauled up the bucket with her beak. Jesse and his father had taught her this trick. It was Jesse's favorite.

"Now, let's go over our plan again," Jesse said. "Zenith and I will hide, and as soon as you see someone acting funny—"

"Behaving suspiciously," Walter put in. He watched more TV than Jesse did.

"You know what I mean. If you see anything that looks like shoplifting, get the message to me."

"We'll need our walkie-talkies," Walter reminded him.

Jesse scooted under his bed. "Here's one," he called out.

"Look around for another one," Walter told him. "I think I left mine over here."

"You're right." Jesse crawled out holding two walkie-talkies covered with dust balls. "Let's make sure the batteries still work." He handed one to Walter and then tried his out. "Testing. Testing."

"Testing," Zenith echoed. "One, two, three."

Walter spoke into his walkie-talkie. "This thing works, but is your plan going to? That's what I want to know."

"I keep telling you, it's bound to work. When you spot a shoplifter, you follow her around until you see her take something and then—"

"How do you know it will be a woman?" Walter interrupted.

"Because I'm going to be hiding inside that big round rack of women's bathrobes by the escalator. That's where our command post will be. And most of the shoppers around there are women."

Jesse paused for a moment as he refilled Zenith's bucket. "So when I get the word from you, I'll come charging out—"

"With Zenith?" Walter broke in again.

"No. I'll leave her behind on top of the bathrobe rack." Jesse went on with the plan. "After you point out the shoplifter, I'll arrest her."

"Tell her you're making a citizen's arrest," Walter suggested. "I saw someone do that on TV."

"That sounds good," Jesse said. "Then I'll tell her to follow me to the manager's office."

"What if she won't do that?" Walter asked.

"That's where you come in," Jesse said. "She's probably going to try to escape. You have to keep her from getting to the escalator."

Now came Jesse's favorite part of the plan. "I'll grab her arm and start yelling for help. When Zenith hears that, she'll come swooping down from the sky—"

Walter started laughing. "The sky?"

"I mean the bathrobe rack," said Jesse

quickly. "With Zenith and me hanging on to her, that shoplifter will be *begging* to turn herself in. You've seen Superbird in action."

They looked over at Zenith. She wasn't in action right now. Sleepy from the afternoon heat and the popcorn, she had flown back to her cage for a nap. In the cage was a towel hanging from a hook. Zenith was wrapping it around herself with her beak. She liked to sleep that way.

Walter grinned at Jesse. "I hope she doesn't wrap herself in a bathrobe at the store and go to sleep."

"Maybe I did give her too much to eat," Jesse admitted. "But don't worry. She'll be as strong as an eagle tomorrow."

"Did your mother say we could go for sure?" Walter asked.

"Not yet, but she will," said Jesse confidently. "Last night Zenith flew up on top of

the curtain rod and chewed a big hole in the drapes. "Now Mom *really* wants her wings clipped."

Just then they heard the front door slam. "That's Lucas," Jesse said as he rushed out of the room.

Mrs. Beeman had said she would talk to Lucas about the trip to the mall. That's what she was doing, while Jesse eavesdropped from the top of the stairs.

"Aww, Mom," Lucas said, his voice higher than usual. "What if my friends see me? There I'll be, with this weird little kid with a bird on his shoulder."

"Zenith will *not* be on his shoulder," said Mrs. Beeman firmly. "You know we never take her outside that way."

Lucas grumbled on. "Well, anyway, I'll bet Walter will be wearing his propeller hat."

At this point, Jesse galloped down the stairs. He knew how to change Lucas's mind. "Guess what?" he announced. "Marvin's Starcade at the mall has an incredible new video game. Somebody at school told me about it."

"Attack of the Mutant Men?" asked Lucas instantly.

"Even better—Blackbeard's Revenge."

Lucas hesitated. "Okay, I'll take you to the mall. Just make sure Walter doesn't wear that stupid hat."

"Don't worry—he won't," Jesse promised as he raced back up the stairs.

CHAPTER 6

SUSPICIOUS BEHAVIOR

You're still too close to me," Lucas complained. "Stay here and count to fifty. Then start walking."

"That's fine with us. We don't want to walk with you anyway." Jesse began to count. By the time he finished, Lucas was a block ahead of them.

It was Friday at last, and they were on their way to the mall. Jesse was all prepared. He had his walkie-talkie in the pocket of his sweatshirt, along with some treats for Zenith. And, of course, he had Zenith. It wasn't quite as wonderful as he had hoped, though. She wasn't riding proudly on his shoulder. Instead, his mother had put Zenith in a large paper bag. It was stapled shut at the top and had holes punched in the sides for air.

Zenith didn't mind traveling this way. She talked to herself contentedly, running through her favorite sayings. "Hey, birdbrain. Want a cup of coffee? Too hot! Happy New Year! Happy New Year!"

The people they passed looked at the bag curiously. One man said, "Well, Happy New Year to you, too."

Besides his walkie-talkie, Walter was carrying as much defense equipment as he could. He had a bag of pepper, his fossil rock, his horseshoe magnet, and his good-luck penny. The penny had been minted the year he was

born, which made it extra lucky. And for even more protection, he was wearing his new lucky jacket.

"Why did you have to wear that jacket?" Jesse grumbled. "Undercover agents never wear *anything* red."

"I can hold my walkie-talkie under it like this." Walter showed him. "Then nobody can tell I'm using it. Besides, undercover agents don't carry talking paper bags, either."

"That's different," Jesse said, but he scratched on the side of the bag a little. Whenever he did this, Zenith stopped talking.

Lucas was waiting for them at the main entrance. "All right, now. You guys are on your own for an hour and a half," he told them. "I'll meet you by the fountain at five o'clock." Then he turned and headed toward Marvin's Starcade, his pockets jingling with quarters. "Stay on the first level," he yelled back. "And remember—we don't tell Mom that we split up."

As soon as Lucas was out of sight, Jesse and Walter took the glass elevator to the second level.

"An hour and a half," Walter said. "That's not enough time to catch a shoplifter and get Zenith's wings clipped."

"It only takes a few minutes to clip them," Jesse said. "Besides, after we catch a shoplifter, Mom won't care about Zenith's wings. We'll be heroes."

They walked into the Hayes Department Store.

"Hey, birdbrain. Happy New Year!" Zenith squawked.

"Shh, not so loud, Zenith." Jesse scratched on the bag. Now was the time to start blending in with the crowd. And there really *was* a crowd. It was going to be hard to walk through the china department without bumping into people.

"I wonder what's going on," Jesse said.

Walter pointed to a sign near them:

COME SEE TIZANIA THE SORCERESS, AN EXCITING NEW FANTASY FIGURE BY MADAME FABULANA

"My aunt Emiko collects those figures," Walter said.

They studied the picture of the sorceress on the sign. She was dressed in gauzy silver robes. Her high, pointed hat was covered with jeweled stars, and in one hand she held a dazzling crystal globe.

"Is that what all these people are waiting for?" Jesse looked at the long line of impatient-looking people that snaked through the china department. "They must be crazy."

"Oh, I don't know about that," Walter said. "Aunt Emiko says her Fantasy Figures are worth a lot more now than what she paid for them."

"I still think they're crazy," Jesse said. "Let's go. Our command post is this way."

As they were trotting through the boys' department, Jesse glanced over at a group of mannequins. They all had yo-yos. There must have been some kind of motor in the yo-yos —they were going up and down.

"Boy, those dummies are almost real," Jesse said. "But there's something funny about their faces. They look sort of surprised."

"It's the eyebrows—see." Walter raised his until they disappeared under his hair.

Jesse laughed. "That's it. You look just like one now."

On the other side of the boys' department

was the bathrobe rack in women's lingerie. They were almost to their post.

"Happy New Year!" Zenith was talking louder again. Jesse quickly scratched on the bag. "When I get inside our command post, I'll give her some nuts. That will keep her quiet."

"I hope so," Walter said. "The saleswoman over there is staring at us."

Jesse moved behind the rack and waited. As soon as no one was watching, he slipped inside and sat down. Now he was surrounded by fuzzy robes that hung almost to the floor. They were packed tightly together. Most of them were green or maroon. Jesse thought they were ugly. That was good. Nobody would want to buy one. But if they did, they might notice him. Maybe he should have some sort of camouflage just in case someone liked icky-colored bathrobes. He pulled a robe off its hanger and draped it around his shoulders.

Then he opened the paper bag so Zenith could climb out. She perched on his arm and made soft clucking noises. That meant she was glad to see him.

"Good girl," said Jesse as he rubbed her head. He turned on his walkie-talkie. No messages from Walter yet, but Jesse didn't expect to catch a shoplifter in the first ten minutes. It might take half an hour.

He gave Zenith a Brazil nut to keep her busy.

Another five minutes went by. Jesse began to get impatient. "What's going on out there, Walter?"

"Nothing. I mean, everybody's acting normal . . ." Walter's voice faded out.

"I can't hear you," Jesse complained.

"Sorry. My collar got in the way," Walter said. "There is a woman who looks a little suspicious, though."

Jesse perked up. "What's she doing?"

"She keeps looking over at the saleswoman," Walter told him.

Jesse leaned forward and carefully parted the robes to look for Walter. "Where are you now?" he asked.

"I'm in the boys' department—over by the dummies with the yo-yos," Walter said.

Jesse shifted his lookout spot. "Oh, now I see you. Where's the woman?"

"She's by the counter." Jesse saw Walter pointing with his elbow. "The woman carrying a baby in one of those pouches in the front."

"Hmm." Jesse got a quick glimpse of the woman. "That would be a good way to take

things—just stick them in the pouch with the baby." Jesse had another idea. "Hey! I'll bet that's not even a real baby."

"Maybe not," Walter agreed. "No . . . I can see the baby moving around. But I'll keep an eye on her anyway."

Walter moved out of range, and Jesse closed

the robes. Walter sounded as if he was having a good time. Jesse felt a little jealous. But his turn would come when he and Zenith made the arrest.

"Hey, birdbrain," Zenith squawked. She had cracked the Brazil nut at last. Jesse gave her a few grapes to work on. The fuzzy bathrobe was tickling his ear. As he tugged at the robe, some of the green fuzz came off in his fingers. He blew it away and then looked at his watch. It was four-twenty.

"Uh-oh! You won't believe this." Walter sounded alarmed. "I think I just saw your neighbor, Mrs. Orewiler."

"You probably did," Jesse said. He didn't seem concerned about it. "She's here all the time. Mom says she practically lives at the mall."

"If she sees me, she'll want to know where you are," Walter pointed out.

Jesse hadn't thought of that. He began to worry. "Whatever you do, don't tell her *anything*." But he knew how nosy Mrs. Orewiler was. She would worm it out of Walter somehow. And then she would make a big fuss. There would be no chance of catching a shoplifter after that.

"Just stay out of her way, Walter," Jesse told him.

"What do you think I'm trying to do?" Walter said. "But she keeps changing her direction. Oh, no! She's heading straight toward me!"

TALKING BATHROBES

Jesse did some fast thinking. "Quick, Walter! Get up on that platform behind you and do your dummy act."

Walter leaped up and then froze into position. He looked just like the store mannequins beside him—except he didn't have a yo-yo.

"Perfect. Now hold it." Jesse watched Mrs. Orewiler walk right past Walter. She didn't even look up.

"It worked!" Walter was jubilant as he jumped down from the platform.

But their troubles weren't over yet.

"Bad news, Jesse," Walter told him. "She's heading your way."

Jesse could see her coming. And if anyone

would like icky-green bathrobes, it would be Mrs. Orewiler. He closed his peephole and waited.

Walter continued to report. "She's pawing through some stuff on the table next to you." A moment later he said, "Now she's looking at some other bathrobes."

Jesse began to relax. Maybe Mrs. Orewiler would buy one of those other robes and go away.

Even before Walter warned him, Jesse knew she had switched her attention. One of the tightly packed robes was yanked out of his rack.

"Are these robes on sale?" It was her voice. He could tell Zenith had recognized it, too. She stopped nibbling on the grapes and looked up.

"I thought I saw them advertised in the paper," Mrs. Orewiler went on.

"Yes—they've been marked twenty-five per-cent off."

"She's talking to the saleswoman," Walter said.

"Not so loud," Jesse whispered into his walkie-talkie. "She might hear you."

Zenith was starting to mutter to herself. Softly at first, then a little more loudly, she said, "Sasha. Sasha, come here."

"Shh!" Jesse dumped out the rest of the Brazil nuts. That didn't work. Zenith was more interested in talking than eating. "Sasha! Come here, Sasha!"

Although Walter couldn't hear Zenith, he knew something was wrong. "What's going on? Your neighbor is just standing there, staring at the rack."

Jesse didn't answer. He was too busy trying to quiet Zenith.

"Do you hear something?" Mrs. Orewiler

asked. "It sounds like a voice is coming from inside those bathrobes."

"I'm afraid I don't hear anything," the saleswoman said.

Zenith finally calmed down and began to work on the Brazil nuts.

Then Jesse heard a new woman's voice. "Excuse me—is that one you're holding an extra-large?"

"No, it's marked medium," Mrs. Orewiler answered. "I'm looking for an extra-large, too," she went on in a fretful voice. "But I don't see one in this color."

"That's always the way it is with sales." It was *another* new voice.

Jesse began to get alarmed. Mrs. Orewiler seemed to have started a stampede on these awful bathrobes. Pretty soon, the rack would be picked clean and there he'd be—in plain sight. He crouched lower and pulled his camouflaging robe over his head.

A few more bathrobes were removed, and then Jesse heard Mrs. Orewiler say, "I know why these robes are on sale. The fuzz is coming right off—look."

Good. Maybe nobody will want to buy one now, thought Jesse. He checked his watch. It was already four-thirty, and they still hadn't caught any shoplifters.

Two more messages came through from Walter. "Mrs. Orewiler is leaving," he reported. That was a relief. And then, "Hey, remember that woman with the baby? I saw her again. And I think she just stuffed a pair of socks into the pouch with the baby."

"Is she coming this way?" Jesse asked.

"Maybe," Walter answered. "I'll let you know."

Hooray! Their plan might work after all. "In a few minutes, we're going to catch our first shoplifter," Jesse whispered to Zenith.

"Excuse me. Coming through." It was a man's voice. Immediately after Jesse heard that, something rammed into the bathrobe rack.

"What was *that?*" Jesse asked.

"Two guys were moving a rack of coats," Walter told him. "They bumped into your rack."

The bathrobes were still swaying violently. Zenith fluttered her wings in alarm and then began to climb up through the robes. Jesse grabbed for her, but he was too late. As soon as she had cleared the rack, she took off, squawking loudly.

A woman screamed, and Jesse could hear other voices talking excitedly.

"What is it?"

"Looks like a parrot."

"Where did it come from?"

Grabbing the paper bag and his walkie-talkie, Jesse scrambled out. He had a quick glimpse of Walter's face. Walter looked as if he had swallowed his own fossil rock.

Jesse tried to move and then realized he still had a bathrobe wrapped around him. He threw it off and ran after Zenith. She wasn't flying very high, but she was staying just out of reach. That was good. Jesse wanted to be the one to catch her. But he wasn't the only person chasing her. Twice he collided with a tall saleswoman.

"Is that your parrot?" she asked him the second time. He didn't answer.

Zenith finally perched on a high store display of giant autumn leaves. She was still shrieking steadily.

"Call the maintenance department," the

tall saleswoman said. "Tell them to send someone with a ladder."

Walter ran over to Jesse. They looked up at Zenith. She was at least six feet above their heads.

"Boy, are we in trouble," Walter said.

"Not if we can get her down before they bring the ladder," Jesse told him. "Nobody knows who we are except Mrs. Orewiler." He looked around quickly. "And I don't see her anywhere. Come on, Walter. Let's get Zenith down."

"Wait till she's looking at us." Zenith was nibbling at a huge plastic leaf in the display.

"Okay, *now!*" Walter grabbed Jesse's arm.

"Help! Help me!" yelled Jesse.

"This had better work fast," Walter said.

It took Zenith longer than usual, but finally she flew down to Jesse's rescue. Walter dived under a counter to get out of her way. She lit on Jesse's shoulder and kept up her earsplitting shrieks.

The tall saleswoman came over to him. She looked half angry and half amused. Jesse could hardly hear her over Zenith's racket, but he thought she said something about an "amazing parrot."

"I know," he answered proudly.

Another saleswoman was coming toward them now, leading a man with a ladder. She didn't look amused at all.

"Let's get out of here," Jesse said. "Where's that paper bag?"

"I've got it." Walter held it out. "You dropped it over there."

Jesse tucked Zenith inside the bag, and they raced to the escalator.

CITIZEN'S ARREST

As Jesse and Walter leaped off the escalator at the bottom, Jesse glanced back. He saw the angry saleswoman at the top. And she saw him. She stepped on and started walking down briskly. Just their luck, Jesse thought. Most grown-ups didn't walk the escalators—they rode them.

"Come on, Walter! This way!"

They dashed past counters piled high with handbags and then through the cosmetics department. Here the crowd was thicker, and they had to slow down. Walter was sprayed accidentally as they passed a woman sampling perfume.

"That stuff smells awful," he gasped.

After that, they were in the men's department. There weren't many shoppers in this area. It was easy to slip into one of the empty dressing rooms to hide. Out of breath, they collapsed against the wall.

"Do you think she followed us?" Walter asked.

"I don't know," Jesse said. "Take a look."

Walter peeked out and then ducked back inside. "She's still there," he said. "Now she's talking to one of the salesmen. I hope he didn't see us come in here." Walter sat down and sniffed at his sleeve unhappily. "Whew! I smell like perfume." He rubbed his sleeve hard on the carpet.

"You sure do," Jesse agreed. Looking down, he saw that he still had green fuzz from the bathrobes sticking to him. He flopped on the floor next to Walter and picked a few pieces of fuzz off his sweatshirt.

Then he opened the bag to see how Zenith was doing. Being in the dark had calmed her down a little, but she didn't sound happy. "Let me out of here! Let me out!"

"You can come out for a few minutes," Jesse told her. She climbed up his arm to his shoulder. He found an old ball-point pen top in the corner and gave it to her. She usually loved to tear them apart. But even that didn't cheer her up.

Jesse didn't feel any happier than Zenith. All of their undercover detective plans had failed. "Where did that woman with the baby go?" he asked Walter.

"You ran right by her when you were chasing

Zenith," Walter said. "I didn't see her after that."

This time Jesse checked to see if the saleswoman was still there. "She's gone," he reported. "It's getting late. We might as well take Zenith to the pet shop." Zenith squawked angrily as he put her back in the bag.

They left the dressing room and headed for the department store exit that led out into the mall area. The pet shop was five or six stores away. But before they reached the exit, a woman brushed past them, nearly knocking Zenith's bag out of Jesse's hand. She was wearing a black coat and carrying a big, square package. In her black high-heeled boots, she rushed through the door and disappeared into the crowd of shoppers outside.

"She nearly ran over us," Walter fumed.

"Stop! Wait!" Now a large man wearing a baseball cap tore by and barreled out the door.

Jesse's eyes lit up. "No wonder she was in such a hurry," he said. "She's a shoplifter, that's what!"

Jesse quickly tucked Zenith's bag under his arm so she wouldn't bounce around. Then he started to run. "Come on! She's going to get away," he yelled back to Walter.

"Are you sure about this?" Walter was panting as he tried to keep up.

"Didn't you see how guilty she looked?" Jesse said.

"All I saw was the back of her head," Walter pointed out, but he kept on running.

For a few minutes, they lost sight of the man in the baseball cap. They paused by the fountain in the middle of the mall and looked around. Then Jesse saw him standing by the glass elevator. He was looking around, also, not sure which way to go.

"There he is! There's the store detective!" Jesse shouted.

"He doesn't look much like one," Walter said.

"He's undercover—like us," Jesse told him. "I think he's lost the woman. We'll have to help him find her."

Jesse handed the bag with Zenith to Walter. Then he scrambled to the top of the low wall that surrounded the fountain. From there he could see over the heads of the crowd.

Walter was ready to give up. All he could think of was the wonderful aroma coming from the doughnut shop near them. It almost drowned out the smelly perfume on his jacket. "That woman is probably halfway home by now," he said.

"Wrong again. There she is!" Jesse had spotted the woman in black by the exit that led to the parking structure. He jumped down from the wall and ran over to the man in the baseball cap. Tugging hard on the man's arm, he pointed. "She's over there—going out the exit."

The man gave him a strange look. "How do you . . ." he began. Then he stopped talking and rushed toward the exit. For a big man, he moved pretty fast. Jesse had a hard time keeping up with him as he dodged around the wave of incoming shoppers.

Walter had an even harder time. He was still carrying Zenith, and he didn't want to shake her around too much.

"Hurry up, Walter!" Jesse yelled. He ran through the exit into the parking structure. It looked enormous to him. There were five levels for parking, counting the roof. How could they find out which level the woman's car was on?

The man in the baseball cap seemed to be wondering the same thing. Finally, he made a decision and headed up the ramp to the second level.

"I'll check around down here," Jesse called to him. The man glanced back in surprise. He didn't seem to realize that Jesse was helping him. Some detective! Why, he wouldn't even know where the shoplifter was if it hadn't been for me, Jesse thought.

Turning left, Jesse scanned the row of parked cars. A few cars cruised past him slowly, hunting for parking spaces. But no woman in black. Jesse moved on to another row of cars and looked up and down. At the far end, he saw her, tapping along in her high-heeled boots. She was still in a big hurry.

Walter was right behind him now. Jesse could hear Zenith's loud protests. "Let me out of here! Let me out!" He grabbed Zenith's bag from Walter and opened it. Jesse wanted her to be riding on Walter's shoulder when he made the arrest. That way, she could fly to his rescue.

Zenith looked very fierce when she put her head out of the bag. Her feathers were sticking out at all angles. As soon as she was on Walter's shoulder, she began to poke them back into place with her beak.

"Ow! Does she always dig her claws in like this?" Walter asked uneasily.

Jesse didn't answer. He was too busy thinking about capturing the shoplifter. They were on their own now, since he didn't know where the detective was. "Get that bag of pepper ready," he told Walter. "We may need it." Then he raced ahead again.

Walter followed at a fast walk, with one hand holding on to Zenith's feet.

The woman had reached her car. She was balancing the package against the door as she hunted through her purse. Jesse was near enough to hear her talking to herself. "Now where did I put them . . ." In a moment she would find her keys and get away. Jesse decided not to warn her that she was under arrest. He'd go straight to the second part of the plan— Zenith.

Jesse waited for Walter to catch up, and then he moved in closer to the woman. When he was only a few feet away from her, he began to yell. "Save me! Help! Help! Save me, Zenith!"

The woman looked so astonished, she nearly dropped her package. "What are you doing?"

"Help! HELP!"

"Stop that yelling!"

Jesse grabbed the woman's arm to make Ze-

nith think he was being attacked. The woman
jerked away from him. "You must be crazy!"
she said as she dumped her purse out on the
car hood. Clutching the package under one
arm, she searched frantically for her car keys.

Zenith still hadn't budged from Walter's shoulder. What was wrong with her? Jesse wondered. In desperation, he stepped up the volume. "OWWWWOWWWW!" His howling boomed and echoed around the parking structure.

That did it. Zenith left Walter and headed straight toward them.

"Help!" the woman shrieked. She dropped her package and threw up her arms to protect herself.

"Come on, Superbird!" Jesse yelled.

But Zenith didn't lay a feather on the woman. She zoomed over Jesse's head and kept on flying. Finally she settled on one of the overhead pipes nearby.

Jesse couldn't believe it. He had never thought that Zenith would fly away from him.

But she had.

ZENITH, BACK COME

Jesse called and called to Zenith. She ignored him. Walter pretended to fight with him, and Jesse hollered for help. But it didn't work this time. She wasn't even looking down at them. Instead, she kept turning her head, trying to see all around her. Jesse began to realize why she was acting so strangely. She was frightened. His brave Zenith was frightened.

The woman had picked up her package and

was shaking it gently. "This had better not be broken," she warned Jesse. "What on earth were you trying to do?"

Jesse hardly heard her question. He was so afraid that Zenith would fly farther away. The thought made him panicky. He searched his pockets for what was left of Zenith's treats. Maybe he could coax her down with some Brazil nuts. If he could get up closer to her, she would be able to see the nuts better.

"Do you mind if I stand on top of your car?" Jesse asked the woman.

"I certainly *do* mind," she said indignantly.

Jesse turned to Walter. "Maybe if I stood on your shoulders . . ." he began.

At that moment, the man in the baseball cap came puffing up. "There you are," he said to the woman. "I've been hunting all over." Then he saw Jesse. "You again!" the man said in surprise.

"Do you *know* these crazy children?" the woman asked. She had to raise her voice, since Jesse and Walter were calling to Zenith.

The man shook his head. "I never saw them before today."

Somewhere nearby, a car tooted its horn. The noise echoed loudly in the parking structure. Zenith squawked in alarm and her eyes flashed.

The man looked up. "What a beautiful bird," he said. "Where did it come from?"

"She's mine," Jesse answered proudly. "Will you help me get her down?" Maybe he could stand on the man's shoulders. Or, even better, Walter could stand on the man's shoulders and Jesse could stand on Walter's.

"I'll try to help you," the man said and then turned to the woman. "Don't leave yet, Mrs. Mayfield. I'm sure we can work something out."

"Hey, how come he knows her name?" Walter whispered to Jesse. "And why isn't she trying to make a getaway?"

Before Jesse could answer, a car alarm went off. It beeped and honked and then became an earsplitting siren. Zenith let out a scream almost as loud as the alarm. Her eyes flashed again, and she took off. She flew swiftly to the ramp and on up to the next level. In a moment she had disappeared from sight.

"Quick! This way." Jesse dashed to a stairway near them. Walter trotted after him. When they reached the second level, they stopped.

"Where did she go?" Jesse looked around wildly.

"This is a big building," Walter said. "She could be anywhere."

"We've got to find her," Jesse told him desperately.

They heard a distant squawk behind them and spun around.

"Hey, I think I see her over there." Walter pointed straight ahead.

"You're right," Jesse said. "Come on."

As they ran past parked cars, Jesse's heart was racing faster than his feet. He was feeling more panicky by the minute. If only this had happened inside the store, he thought. Zenith would finally get tired and land somewhere. The parking structure, on the other hand, was open on all four sides. Sooner or later, she would fly outside.

Jesse stopped suddenly to let a car pass. Walter crashed into him. The car moved slowly as it waited for another car to pull out of a parking space. Jesse and Walter had to backtrack around it. This only took a moment, but in that moment, Zenith disappeared again.

They stood still, panting and wondering

which way to go. Then Walter said, "There she is. She's flying up the ramp." They ran behind her and sprinted up the ramp to the third level.

There they stopped again and listened for Zenith. Jesse's heart was hammering in his ears so loudly, it was hard to hear. This was the worst thing that had ever happened to him. He couldn't hear Zenith and he couldn't see her. He might *never* see her again. He remembered stories he had heard about parrots that flew away and didn't come back.

"Stop breathing so hard," Jesse panted. "I'm trying to listen."

"I can't help it," Walter protested.

"Do you hear anything?" asked Jesse.

"Too much," Walter said. "Doors slamming, people talking, cars moving."

"Well, we can't just stand here," Jesse said. "Let's go."

They looked down every aisle of cars as they passed.

"I hope she's still flying," Jesse said. "It'll be easier to spot her."

Suddenly Jesse was convinced they were going in the wrong direction. "Let's turn around and go back."

But they hadn't gone more than a few car lengths the other way when he had the same feeling again.

"Stop!" he shouted.

"Make up your mind, will you," Walter snapped. Then, seeing the misery on his friend's face, he added, "Hey, don't worry. We'll find her. Why don't we split up?"

"Good idea," said Jesse gratefully. "I'll go this way."

As he trotted along, Jesse made promises to himself. He would never be careless with Zenith again. Never. And he would buy a leash for her foot, if he ever took her out again.

Jesse was next to an open side of the building now. He could see the trees outside. If he were a parrot, that's where he would go. Jesse moved from a trot to a gallop.

Off to his left, he heard people talking loudly. They sounded nearby but just out of

sight. Maybe they're excited because they saw a parrot fly by, Jesse thought.

He raced to the next row of cars and skidded around the corner. There she was, still flying. He couldn't have missed her. Two little girls were pulling on their mother's arm and pointing at Zenith.

Walter must have heard all the commotion, too. Jesse saw him at the other end of the row of cars. They both yelled, "Zenith!" and began to run.

Zenith was heading for the open side now. Jesse was running so hard, he didn't have enough breath to shout. Should he keep running or stop to call her?

She had only two more aisles of cars to cross, and she would be outside. Jesse decided to take a chance on calling. He stopped, gulped for air, and yelled, "Zenith, come back!" When that didn't stop her, he tried "Back come, Zenith!" Walter had always told him that saying something backward made it come true. Who knows—it might work.

But it didn't. Zenith flew on. In another moment, she would be in the trees.

Just then, a high van moved down the aisle in front of her, and she swerved to avoid it.

Now she was heading back toward Jesse. She passed him and landed two cars away, on the handlebars of a motorcycle. Jesse couldn't believe it. If only she didn't move before he could reach her.

He tried Walter's method again, just in case it worked after all. "Move don't, Zenith," he said as he raced over to the motorcycle. He could feel her trembling when he picked her up. She seemed as happy to see him as he was to see her.

Walter ran up. "Boy, it's lucky she stopped," he panted.

"Yeah," Jesse agreed. Maybe it had been luck. He would never know for sure, but he wouldn't make fun of Walter's ideas again.

GREEN FUZZ

After Jesse coaxed Zenith into the shopping bag, they went down the stairs to the first level.

The shoplifter was still there, and so was the detective. He gave Jesse a big smile. "I'm glad to see you've caught your parrot."

"*Never* bring a sensitive bird like that to a shopping mall," the woman said, backing away nervously. "Don't come any closer now."

Then she handed her package to the man.

"I'll have to make sure it's not broken," he said. He took a large box out of the shopping bag.

"Aren't you going to arrest her?" Jesse burst out.

The man looked startled. "Why would I do that?"

"I told you—these two are completely nuts," the woman said.

"But she stole that," Jesse insisted.

"What!" The woman was outraged. "I paid good money for it."

"Well, if she's not a shoplifter, why were you chasing her?" Jesse asked.

"Because she bought the last Fantasy Figure." The man opened the box, and Jesse could see what was inside. The light wasn't very bright, but still the stars gleamed in the tall, silvery hat of Tizania the sorceress. Her crystal globe sparkled.

Jesse had never felt so disappointed. He thought of all the trouble he had gone through. He had nearly lost Zenith for nothing.

"I waited for hours in that line . . ." the man said.

"Well, so did I," the woman interrupted.

"Yes, but I was ahead of you," the man reminded her. "You promised you would save my place when I had to leave to call the office. And then I came back and found you running off with the last Fantasy Figure."

The woman defended herself. "You were gone for a long time."

"I had to make several calls," the man admitted. "But you knew how much I wanted to buy this. It's my wife's birthday tomorrow, and this is all she's asked for."

"Well, it's hers now," the woman said crossly. "So don't make such a fuss."

"Yes, after I gave you twice what you paid for it," the man grumbled. "But it's worth it. Alice is just going to love this one. It will be the showpiece of her collection."

Then the woman who wasn't a shoplifter got into her car and drove off.

The two boys walked back to the mall with the man who wasn't a store detective. Jesse was still disappointed, but Zenith was safe and in her traveling bag again. That's all that mattered.

"I'm going to have this gift wrapped," the man said happily. "I can't wait to see Alice's face when she opens it. Maybe I should buy her some perfume, too."

Jesse grinned and whispered to Walter, "Gee, I wonder what made him think of that?"

Walter held his sleeve up to his nose and sniffed. "I think it's fading," he said hopefully.

Jesse and Walter waved good-bye to the man and began to walk toward the fountain.

"It's past five-thirty," Walter said. "But I don't see Lucas waiting for us."

"We're lucky—he's late, too. Maybe we can still get Zenith's wings clipped." Jesse turned and raced toward the pet shop.

Once there, they waited impatiently for the clerk to clip Zenith's wing feathers. Then Jesse tried to put Zenith back into her bag. She protested loudly.

"Why don't you let her ride on your shoulder," Walter said. "She can't fly anymore."

Just what he had always wanted, Jesse thought with regret. But not now. He wasn't going to take any chances. Gently, he coaxed Zenith into the bag. He had finally succeeded when he heard a familiar voice behind him.

"I don't see any Tasty Bones on the shelf. They're Sasha's favorite treat."

It was Mrs. Orewiler.

"I'm afraid we're out of those," the clerk told her.

"Oh, Sasha will be so disappointed," Mrs. Orewiler said, turning around and bumping into Jesse.

"Jesse Beeman," she said in surprise. "Is your mother at the mall?"

"No, we're here with Lucas," Jesse answered.

"I suppose that dreadful bird of yours is in there," Mrs. Orewiler said, looking at the bag.

Zenith had been quiet, but now she started to squawk. "Stop that! Let me out of here!"

The clerk laughed.

"Believe me, it's not funny living next door to that bird," Mrs. Orewiler said, giving Jesse a disapproving look. Then she looked again, this time at the top of his head. She leaned forward and picked a little bit of green fluff out of his hair. Jesse couldn't believe it. He still had fuzz from the bathrobes sticking to him.

"Now, where have I see this before?" Mrs. Orewiler wondered.

"Sasha! Come here, Sasha!" Zenith's voice

was muffled by the bag, but she still sounded like Mrs. Orewiler.

Jesse and Walter said good-bye hastily. When they glanced back, Mrs. Orewiler was staring after them with a thoughtful look on her face.

"I think she knows you were inside that rack," Walter whispered.

"Yeah," Jesse said uneasily. "I hope she doesn't tell Mom."

They headed toward the fountain.

"I still don't see Lucas," Walter said. There was no answer from Jesse. Walter turned and saw Jesse several stores behind, staring into a jewelry store window.

Walter retraced his steps. "Hey, come on," he said.

Jesse motioned to him to keep quiet. "Guess who I saw go in here," he whispered. "The woman with the baby."

They both looked through the window. They could see the woman, trying on jewelry. She was wearing a sparkly necklace and admiring a gold ring on her finger.

The clerk behind the counter wasn't looking

her way. He was busy with a display of charm bracelets.

Jesse and Walter watched the woman put the necklace back but not the ring. She slipped that into the baby carrier. Her baby yawned and wiggled around. It must be getting pretty lumpy in there, Jesse thought.

The woman moved slowly around to the other side of the counter and began to try on earrings.

Jesse whispered softly. "Did you see that? We've got to do something." Quickly, Jesse ran through possibilities in his mind. They couldn't use Zenith this time. He wasn't going to make that mistake again.

"We'll go in there and tell her we're making a citizen's arrest," Jesse said excitedly. "You get on one side, and I'll be on the other. One of us should try to block the door. No . . .

wait. I've got a better idea. Maybe there's some way I can send a message to a store detective's walkie-talkie with this one." Jesse set Zenith's bag next to the wall and tugged his walkie-talkie out of his pocket. "It might work, if there's a detective nearby."

Walter didn't answer. He walked into the store.

"Wait!" Jesse hissed after him.

Walter went directly to the counter. Jesse saw the clerk lean over to listen to Walter and then glance back over his shoulder at the woman. She was just stashing a pair of earrings in the baby carrier. Realizing that the clerk was watching her, she backed away from the counter quickly. Then she broke into a run.

At first, it looked as if she would make it through the doorway, but Jesse was in her way. He was leaping up and down, waving his arms and shouting, "Stop!"

Zenith shrieked from the bag nearby. "Happy New Year! Happy New Year!"

The woman stopped for a moment. She looked amazed. Then, before she could dodge around Jesse, the clerk came up behind her.

"Not so fast," the clerk said. "You'll have to talk to the security guards. I've just called them." And as soon as he finished saying that, two uniformed guards hurried into the room.

"Boy, that was quick," Jesse said admiringly. He and Walter watched the arrest. The clerk must have told the guards what the boys had done. "Nice work!" one of them said as they left with the shoplifter between them. "I wish we had you two around here all the time," the other one said.

"Wow!" Jesse yelled as soon as the guards were out of sight. "We really did it!" He snatched up Zenith's bag. "Now let's get home and type up those business cards."